# ZEEK'S JOURNEY TO FREEDOM

# SAM PEMBERTON

Publishing Coordinator – Sharon Kizziah-Holmes
Cover Artist – Sandi Lemarr

Paperback-Press
an imprint of A & S Publishing
Paperback Press, LLC
Springfield, Missouri

ISBN -13: 978-1-960499-37-0

# DEDICATION

In Memory of Nancy B. Dailey

What can I say about Nancy…from the first time we met and talked about her helping with my books, she was a joy. She lent me her talent as an author, editor and writing coach since that day.

Unfortunately, Nancy lost her battle with ALS soon after she finished working on this story. Without her help, this book may never have come to life.

Rest in peace, my friend. You are missed.

# ACKNOWLEDGEMENTS

Once again, I'd like to thank Sandi Lemarr for the great job she did painting the image for this book cover. Your time and efforts are appreciated.

Sharon Kizziah-Holmes, as always, you are the one that pulls it all together. You know you're my favorite publishing coordinator. I trust your abilities and your advice. Thank you for all you do to make everything as good as it can be and for making this authors publishing dream come true.

Thanks to my wife Pat for putting up with the hours I spend sitting at the computer writing. You're my number one fan and I can't tell you how much I appreciate your hard work on proofing my work. I thank God for you daily.

# CHAPTER 1

It was a warm September day in Searcy County, Arkansas. The county, organized in 1838, had just moved the county seat from Raccoon Springs to Marshall, Arkansas. The county was booming in the 1850s. The courthouse, built on a hill between the Boston Mountain range to the south and the Ozark Mountain range to the north, was finished.

It was a Saturday, and as usual, the town was crowded. This time the crowd was larger than normal. No one would notice the bright yellow maple trees or the deep red of the gum trees. The beauty of the leaves turning to their fall colors was not the main attraction. The crowd, gathering around the courthouse, came because of the hearing to determine the freedom of one of their neighbors.

Zeek Mathews and his wife, Vida, had been their neighbors for over thirty years. She was a full- blooded Indian, and he appeared to be a rather dark-complexioned white man with probably some Indian blood, too. They found it hard to believe that Zeek Matthews was a runaway slave, as claimed by a plantation owner.

Zeek and Vida had raised their children and were part of the community. Their children were now married with children of their own, and were members of different families from the area. No one had ever considered their race. Color had never been mentioned.

Some of the crowd were ready to condemn Zeek. A larger percentage were there to support him. The courthouse was crowded. People were crammed in, ready to listen to the hearing. The large overflow crowd stood outside in the bright sunlight and warmth of the early fall day. A large group had gathered at the south entrance to the building. They watched as Zeek Matthews, Ethan Massey, Noah Sitton and his father, along with Earl Massey, went into the basement. Zeek's lawyer, Joel Bratton, had an office located there.

They watched as Zeek walked emotionlessly. While he looked serious, he did smile when one of his friends yelled, "Hang in there, Zeek!"

The crowd couldn't hear the proceedings inside. They knew it was special, and they could hear the passionate presentation being made to the court. The loud, fervent speech was that of the attorney for the plantation presenting the claim for the ownership of Zeek, a man who had lived peaceably as a free man for over thirty years. The crowd could only imagine how Zeek was reacting to the presentation of the attorney.

As Zeek listened, he remembered his beginning. He knew he was the son of a white man. He also knew that the plantation owner was his grandfather. He knew his mother was half Choctaw and half black. She was still a slave, the property of the Matthews Plantation in Alabama.

Zeek was tall and angular, like his father. He spent his early childhood in the kitchen area and the vegetable garden. He could remember when his father came and visited the living quarters of the plantation.

Ezekiel, from the Bible, was the name chosen by his mother. She had learned to read after the plantation owner's wife brought a recipe book from Europe. His mother had been taught to read to enable her to cook the recipes selected by her master and his wife.

The plantation owners knew that Zeek's mother was the daughter of a Choctaw man. The Indian brave would sneak onto the plantation to see her mom. It was obvious who the father was when she was born with olive skin, a smooth copper color, rather than the heavily black-pigmented skin of the African slaves.

The typical age for black slaves to be bred was fourteen to fifteen years old, and it was supposed to be by the sire selected by the plantation owner. Zeek's grandmother had disregarded this, and had allowed the Choctaw man to become the father.

Zeek's mother had been raised with Caleb Matthews, the son of the plantation owner. It was as if they were siblings. Caleb was three years older than she was. She loved him very much, first as a playmate, and then when they reached the age of natural attraction, she became his lover.

While she knew her mom's story, she never thought about the consequences of hers and Caleb's relationship. A little over a year after Zeek was born, she realized she was pregnant with another child by Caleb.

She named the second child Ralston, and shortened it to Ross. The young children lived in a separate building, and were taken care of by a nanny assigned to them. No one paid much attention to the boys.

However, one day the master's wife sat and watched them playing in the yard. She was aghast! She suddenly realized that both boys had the characteristics of her son, Caleb. She noticed their lighter skin, the fine texture of their hair, along with mannerisms identical to those of her son.

Later that evening she relaxed on the veranda with her husband, Don Matthews.

"Have you noticed anything different about those two boys of Missy's?" she asked.

"Nah," he said. "I've seen 'em. What about 'em?"

"Next time you see them, look them over. I believe Caleb's their daddy."

Don Matthews laughed loudly. "I wouldn't put it past that boy of ours." He stood up and walked across the veranda to the other end. Turning back to face his wife, he added, "Besides, Missy is a very good-looking little gal with that Choctaw blood mixed with her mama's strong black features."

Mrs. Matthews was bothered by her husband's casual attitude about the situation. They were respected slaveowners. They ran a good plantation, and were third generation owners. There had never been any gossip about their slaves being bred by the white boys living on the plantation.

She knew there were plantations where the slaves were treated as sex objects. The owners and their sons took their pleasures with the young female slaves as they wished. She had also heard the stories about Thomas Jefferson and Sally Russell, his slave, living as man and wife with several children from their relationship. That gossip had been all over the South, discussed at every plantation, but never in public.

She never mentioned the conversation again.

Several months later, her husband brought up the subject as they sat on the veranda.

"I've been watching Missy's boys," he said. After a long pause, he added without any emotion, "They belong to Caleb." He admitted to having two grandsons who were a quarter black, a quarter

Choctaw, and whose father was his son, Caleb Matthews. "They are good-looking little guys," he added.

He left the veranda and walked toward the tool shed.

There was no further discussion until almost a year later. They decided it was time to talk to Caleb. After dinner, they asked Caleb to follow them into the parlor. They sat down, while Caleb remained standing in front of them. He was not nervous. It was as though he expected the conversation to be about his two sons.

Caleb and Missy had several discussions, trying to find a solution to this dilemma. They realized that on a plantation in Alabama in 1800 they did not have any options.

After several moments of silence, Don Matthews said, "Caleb, tell us what you know about Zeek and Ross. Missy's sons?"

With a square set to his jaw and no emotion, Caleb answered. "I am their dad."

Caleb's mother began crying, and left the room, leaving Caleb to answer any further questions that might come from his father.

"You know they are my property," he began, "and as the children of a slave they can never be treated as your children."

Caleb was shocked. His father totally ignored the fact that Zeek and Ross were his grandchildren. They were his flesh and blood, but he chose not to make any reference to that fact.

Caleb left the parlor and walked across the courtyard to the kitchen quarters where Missy was raising their sons. They were growing up in an unusual circumstance. Zeek would be six at his next birthday. Ross had already turned four. Caleb was not yet twenty years old but treated them like his family.

Caleb and Missy knew that someday they would have to answer questions. It was too obvious the boys' father was a white man. Caleb had always loved looking at the little guys. Their skin was just dark enough to show a bit of color. Their hair had enough curl to give it body, and to accent their facial features from black and Choctaw blood. They were two innocent victims.

After the initial conversation, Donald Matthews and his wife decided they were going to send Caleb away to college. They began making plans to send him to Dartmouth in New Hampshire.

Caleb had planned on refusing to go, but when it came time, he realized he was going to be forced. As the son of a plantation owner, he did what he was instructed to do. Caleb and Missy had come to that point where none of the decisions being made were under their control.

## CHAPTER 2

After three weeks in Hanover, New Hampshire, Caleb was still in a state of confusion. He could not clear his mind and process what had happened before he left the Matthews plantation. It was hard for him to understand. He felt helpless and confused when he realized he and Missy didn't have the right to claim the boys as their own. He was still in shock at his father's declaration, "You will do as I say or I will take Missy and the boys to New Orleans and sell them at auction."

Caleb knew the rights of his father as a slave owner. He knew the law said that one-eighth bloodline of a slave meant the person was a colored slave. He knew his sons were one-fourth black. He knew it did not matter who he was, or that he was the white son of the slave owner. He left the plantation knowing he had no other choice. Caleb rode with a load of cotton to the port of Mobile, Alabama. He caught the freighter carrying the cotton to the mills in New Hampshire. He carried with him a letter from his dad, addressed to the president of Dartmouth College.

Caleb had not opened the letter and was not aware of its contents. He sat quietly while the president read the letter. The president stood up. With a solemn expression he said, "Welcome to Dartmouth, Caleb Matthews. I hope you're happy here."

He sat back down and signaled for his secretary to come into the office. They did not discuss any details with Caleb. After a few minutes of discussion, another gentleman came to escort Caleb to his new living quarters.

Caleb recalled all of this as he walked across campus, headed to the cafeteria.

After finishing his evening meal, he retraced his steps back to the dorm. As he laid on the bed and stared at the ceiling, he tried to visualize what was going on back at the plantation. He had no way of knowing what Ross and Zeek were doing. He did not know how things had been explained to them. He wondered if Missy and the boys were doing all right. He wondered if they had been told where he was.

Caleb wrote his mother a letter. He did not offer an apology for Missy and their children. He went into several explanations about how he had never intended to embarrass his parents, or to create problems. He ended the letter by wishing everyone the best, and asked if there was any solution they could think of rather than him having to leave behind his family of two children and a woman he loved.

He did not ask for Missy and the boys' freedom from slavery. In 1807, he knew slavery was a vital part of the plantation economy. Cotton was immensely profitable. Tobacco was, too. All of this wealth was produced by slave labor.

Caleb Matthews' life was at a crossroads. At twenty years old, he had left behind the things he loved. Now he was expected to achieve an education. He vowed he would become a better man. He did not feel guilty, he just continued to feel confused.

## CHAPTER 3

Missy sat, crying. Caleb had been gone for over a year. She had never attempted to explain the situation to the boys. She had started crying when Zeek and Ross came in and told her about a conversation they had overheard.

"The master was yelling," Zeek said, referring to his grandfather, Donald Matthews. He stopped for a minute when he saw the expression on his mother's face, but went on to tell what Donald had said.

"They caused all the trouble they're going to cause!" the plantation owner declared.

Zeek continued to tell about the conversation he had overheard between Donald Matthews and the lady of the plantation. He had no idea of the significance of being their grandchildren. He also didn't understand what trouble they were being accused of.

While he listened, his grandparents discussed Zeek and Ross enough that he came to realize it was because he and Ross were their grandchildren.

"I will take them to the slave auction in New Orleans," Donald Matthews declared loudly.

Missy had to explain to the boys that they were helpless. Caleb had been sent away. She didn't even have any idea where he was. They were the property of the Matthews Plantation, and they had no control over their own destinies.

Zeek and Ross rode in the back of the wagon, sitting close together. They had been loaded into the wagon before daylight. They were not told where they were going. A couple of older slaves rode in the front of the wagon.

"I run off one time too many," one of them said to the other. "That's why I'm going to New Orleans." He looked back at the boys. "Why is dem boys going?"

"Dey da master's grandchildren," said the other one.

Zeek was shocked that the other slaves knew that. He was even more shocked by the question and answer.

The two older slaves continued discussing Donald Matthews being so willing to sell his own flesh and blood at a slave auction. They decided he would sell anybody for a good reason, then added, "He don't even need a reason."

Two days later, the wagon carrying the boys and the other two slaves arrived in New Orleans.

# CHAPTER 4

The two brothers followed their master north, away from the Mississippi River, along a street with several hotels. They headed toward one of the bigger hotels. Zeek looked at the towering buildings, wondering what would happen next.

The older slaves had been left with the New Orleans Trading Company that specialized in marketing slaves. Donald Matthews signed the papers, giving the trading company the right to sell them at auction. They showed no emotion as Donald signed.

Ross whispered, "Why...? Zeek, what's going to become of us?" He followed a couple of steps behind Zeek. They both dropped back several steps behind their grandfather.

They did not understand the concept of being a

grandson. They were too young to understand the process of being sold as a slave. Caleb had been sent away. Mrs. Matthews and their mother had fought over them. They understood they were considered a problem and a possible source of embarrassment. Mrs. Matthews had never given any consideration to the fact that she was also their grandmother.

They were approaching puberty at a very early age. They were growing up fast, both physically and mentally. When they were given jobs with other boys their age, they excelled and did better work than anyone. This just added to the problem. Whoever was supervising them was afraid to discipline them, but at the same time, they never paid them any compliments.

As time passed, the boys showed more of their parentage. Being half white, one quarter black, and one quarter Choctaw had been an excellent choice of breeding if you were trying to create an extremely smart and skilled person.

Donald Matthews arrived at the hotel. He opened the door and motioned for the boys to pass in front of him. They entered a large room, the lobby of one of the nicest hotels in New Orleans. They were greeted by a gentleman in a white suit, carrying a wide-brimmed Panama hat in his left hand. He smiled as he came toward them.

"These the boys you told me about?"

Joseph Reynolds, another plantation owner, shook hands with Donald Matthews.

Zeek wondered what he had told the other plantation owner about them.

Donald pointed to a large sofa beneath the window. The boys sat there. The two plantation owners left the room. The boys sat, alert.

Shafts of light came through the tall windows. The reflections varied in color from the stained-glass parts at the window top. The boys were fascinated with all of the fancy trim work. Huge marble columns stretched all the way to the ceiling. While they looked at the beauty of the lobby, they tried to understand what was happening.

Zeek had no idea how long they sat there. Ross stopped looking around the hotel and stared at the floor. He was anxious and scared, and maybe just confused.

They heard conversation as Donald Matthews and Joseph Reynolds returned from their meeting and came toward them.

"You don't ever tell anybody where these boys came from," Donald Matthews instructed Joseph Reynolds. They shook hands.

The boys' new owner introduced himself to them.

Donald Matthews walked away from his two grandsons without even glancing back over his shoulder. He stepped out into the bright sunshine of Canal Street and walked swiftly out of their sight.

Zeek and Ross had not listened to their new

owner as he introduced himself. They had been busy watching their grandfather walk out of their lives.

Joseph Reynolds and the boys went out the back of the hotel, into an alley. They followed the alley to a carriage, parked and waiting. Zeek noticed the beauty of the carriage with all of its frills, and the matched team of horses hitched to it.

They were greeted by the driver holding the team. He was a well-dressed black man with a special kind of suit Zeek and Ross had never seen before. There was another slave from the Reynolds Plantation who helped the boys get into the back seat of the carriage.

Zeek had tried to take in all the details of the city of New Orleans. He would be nine years old on his next birthday. Ross had just turned seven. They'd never been beaten physically during their time with their mother. If Missy said, "Hush, you boys, hush," they behaved. They didn't understand how they had ever been a problem.

There never were a lot of tears shed during all the ordeals since their father had been sent away. They had no idea why they couldn't live as a family. That question was never answered, or even asked. They were too young to understand the situation.

Donald Matthews was an important man. He was an educated man. He had taken those two boys to New Orleans knowing full well he was their grandfather. He felt like he didn't have a choice.

He sold them to another plantation owner he had gone to college with up north. They were fraternity brothers in college. He had told Joseph Reynolds the entire story of the boys' lives. He started back to his plantation in Alabama, feeling assured that his old fraternity brother would not embarrass him.

He arrived back at the Matthews Plantation without any emotion or regrets. It was just part of being the master of a plantation.

# CHAPTER 5

Ross fell asleep leaning against Zeek. Zeek was wide awake. He watched as the horses traveled at a faster pace than he'd ever gone before. The matched team could canter and then slow down to a smooth fast walk before doing it again. Going north from New Orleans through the small hills on the eastern side of the Mississippi was smooth. The wagon road was well-traveled and well-maintained.

Neither Zeek nor Ross had any idea when they crossed into the state of Mississippi. Neither did they understand the significance of what happened at the hotel. They did know they had been separated from their mother. They also knew they were no longer the property of their grandfather and the Matthews Plantation in Alabama. They were on their way to a new life with a new master of the Reynolds Plantation. He appeared to be a nice man, this Joseph Reynolds.

Sometime during the night, they arrived at the place that was to become their new home. They awoke the next morning in the sleeping quarters of the tack room. It was the room where the harnesses and all the other leather equipment was kept.

A slave a few years older than them came to the door. "You don't get to sleep all day here," he said.

The brothers put their clothes on and followed him across an open courtyard. They entered a room where several people were eating their morning meal. They looked at the tables. Zeek turned to Ross. "What are they eating?"

They didn't recognize any of the food. It was some kind of cake similar to their mother's Johnny cakes, but different. They had been fried, but they were thicker and seemed to be fluffy. When the boys ate them, they found that the cakes were lighter and more like the bread Mrs. Matthews had made.

As they sat down, plates were placed in front of them. A big scoop of hominy grits was splashed on the plate by the servant helping the cook. Before they could take a bite, a spatula of butter was added to the grits. They looked at the others and saw that they used the cakes, or whatever they were, to scoop up the grits and cram them into their mouths.

Zeek thought about how much trouble their mother had gone through to teach them to eat with the silverware Caleb had brought them.

"This ain't nothing like eating at home," Zeek whispered.

He began to eat, using a piece of bread as a ladle to get the grits into his mouth. He tried to keep his hands clean. He also tried to keep his mouth clean, like his dad had taught him when he had been able to sneak into the quarters next to the kitchen and eat with them as a family.

Zeek and Ross listened as Mr. Reynolds explained to the older slave what he wanted them to do.

"I want you to teach them to clean the harness and how to hang it properly as they rub it down with oil," he said. He walked over and picked up a set of hames. "You go ahead and polish the brass," he said as he rubbed the round knobs at the top of each hame.

Mr. Reynolds walked away.

"I am Charles," said the slave, looking at the boys.

"I am Zeek." He turned to his brother. "And this is my brother, Ross."

It had been over a month since that first morning when Charles had them working on the Reynolds Plantation. They had settled into a routine. They would clean harnesses until that job was finished, and then they would work in the toolshed removing broken handles and preparing the axes, hoes, and other metal tools to be sharpened. They also took out the damaged handles, repaired, and replaced them.

One day Zeek overheard Charles telling Mr. Reynolds, "They are the smartest guys I've ever seen." He looked over his shoulder at Zeek, and continued. "If I show them once, I don't have to mention it again."

Mr. Reynolds inspected the harnesses. Every piece was hung perfectly straight. Each of the buckles and the brads in the leather was clean. There was no sign of the oil not being properly wiped into the leather. The bridle bits had been cleaned, and there was no sign of residue from where the horses and mules left stains from chewing grass, or anything else, on the bridles.

He walked to both ends of the rack where the harnesses hung. He then looked at all the other equipment the boys were responsible for cleaning and maintaining.

He left the building and started back toward the main house. He thought about what Don Matthews, his old college friend and fellow plantation owner, had told him about how sure Don was that these boys were his grandchildren by his son and a slave who worked in their plantation kitchen.

He turned and looked back at the building. "If they were mine…," he thought.

He stepped onto the veranda of the main house

and yelled for Mrs. Reynolds to bring him a glass of tea. He had sworn to his friend to never breathe a word of who Zeek and Ross really were, but he wondered how a grandfather could turn his back on his grandsons. He sipped the tea. He didn't have the answer.

He thought about how as the brothers grew older and became exceptional men, showing their white heritage, along with the best traits they inherited from their mother, how would he explain to visitors how he came to own these two slaves?

The master of the Reynolds Plantation was not sure why he had agreed to do this for an old friend.

# CHAPTER 6

Caleb Matthews was in his last year of study at Dartmouth College in Hanover, New Hampshire. He sat at his desk. He read a letter for the third time. He stood up and walked over to close the curtains at the window. The sun shone too brightly for him to continue working.

He glanced out the window at the campus. He had spent four years here studying and trying to forget. The trees were budding, the grass was turning green. He loved the smell of the spring flowers when he walked across campus to his classes. He had done well in his studies, but he was still plagued by his memories from the plantation.

"How did she get my address?" he whispered to himself. He watched the people coming toward his building, then closed the window curtains. He thought about the letter he had just finished reading.

Missy had written a long letter. It was difficult for Caleb to read. Not because of its content, but because of the struggle Misty must've had writing the letter.

He had asked himself how she got his address. The answer to this question was in the first line.

"I copied your address from a letter I read in your mother's office," Missy explained. "She asked me to clean it, and she had left the letter laying on her desk."

Caleb's mind raced as he questioned why his mother appeared to have given his address to Missy.

Missy had written about all the things she remembered since he left. She went into great detail about how well the boys had adjusted for the first couple of years after he was gone. She didn't spend a lot of time writing about them being taken away.

Caleb had adjusted quite well during the past three years. He was now sharing part of his time with a young lady from St. Louis. He could not explain their relationship. To him it was nothing more than a friendship, but he needed a female in his life. He never had any interest in anyone except Missy. He had known his relationship with Missy was not beneficial to either one of them. Their separation had not kept him from loving her and missing their children.

The letter was a complete report, not only about the boys and how well they had done after he left. It also included a complete description of the day Caleb's father loaded the boys into a wagon and left the plantation.

After closing the curtains, Caleb returned to his desk. Picking up the envelope, he stared at the crude writing where Missy had addressed it. Tears filled his eyes when he remembered how Missy was forced to stand several feet away while he was taught to read and write. As a slave, there was no intention for her to ever learn, until Caleb's mother decided she wanted Missy to be able to read the cookbook and prepare the recipes.

Caleb read the letter again. It was easier for him to read the second time, as he was now able to make out all the words. The message hurt even more as he fully understood.

"The master took the boys right after Christmas," Missy had written. "I had no warning," she continued, "he just came in and said he needed the boys to come with him." She went on to write that after he started to leave with them, he turned around and said, "Missy, they won't be back."

Caleb stared at those lines. He tried to imagine the pain Missy had felt. He was sure it was greater than the suffering thoughts he had endured the last three years.

"I don't know if you will get this or if you won't," she had written, "but I feel better sending it to you."

Missy went on to write about the loneliness she had felt since Caleb left. She wrote about the desperation she felt after being left at the plantation without him. She then tried to express the amount of depression she felt after losing the boys. Those lines caused Caleb to wish he had never agreed to come to Dartmouth to go to school. He wished he had agreed to move to the back corner of the plantation and live as a tenant farmer. He wondered if his dad would have allowed him to take his family and share his life with Missy and the boys.

He picked up the letter again and placed it back in the envelope. He was amazed when he noticed the postmark was from St. Louis and was less than two weeks ago.

The letter had been written just after his dad had taken his sons away from their mother. Caleb gritted his teeth and felt disgusted by the circumstances his sons were having to live through.

He thought about all the things he had read about slavery, and how the plantation system created wealth for the southern planters. He thought about all the money that was being spent for his education. And he thought about being the son of privilege since he was the son of an owner of a large plantation.

He placed the letter in his desk drawer underneath a bunch of other papers.

"Caleb," the voice of a young lady at his door said. "I thought you were going to go to dinner with me," she said as he opened the door. She walked past him and turned to face him.

Caleb looked at her. If he had a clear mind and hadn't been worried about the life he had spent three years trying to reconcile, this young lady from St. Louis would've been beautiful. She was five feet, six or seven inches tall, with auburn hair that glistened in the sunlight, accenting her deep brown eyes. She walked with confidence and wore dresses bought in the best dress shops in Boston and St. Louis. She came from a family with money. They were merchants and had made a fortune supplying goods during the expansion of the United States.

Caleb put on his coat and prepared to go out in the cool spring air.

The smell of the flowers and being in the girl's presence could not erase the things he had learned from Missy's letter. He clenched his jaw, trying to adjust his thinking. He was determined to move on. But he would never forget the picture he had in his mind of Missy's description of his father taking their sons away.

## CHAPTER 7

The sun shone brightly on the muddy Mississippi. The steamboat slowly pulled into the dock at Memphis. Zeek and Ross watched as the ship was tied to the dock and the gangplank extended. Zeek followed Ross across the gangplank when they left the boat. They were part of the group of ten slaves from the Reynolds Plantation, provided by Mr. Reynolds. They would be part of the crew surveying Arkansas.

"Ross, can we do this?" Zeek asked as they stepped on the dock. They stopped for a last look at the steamboat which brought them up the river from Natchez.

"How would I know whether we can do this or not?" Ross answered. "We don't even know what the word survey means."

They had been with the survey crew leader since he came to the plantation recruiting men for the survey. Mr. Reynolds had allowed him to visit with several slaves. He selected eight muscular slaves in their mid-twenties before he ever saw Ross and Zeek.

Once he began talking with the boys, it was obvious he knew they were different from the other eight he had selected.

Zeek wondered about the conversation with Mr. Reynolds when the survey chief asked if they could speak privately. He wanted Zeek and Ross as part of the crew. Zeek didn't know if Mr. Reynolds had told him he was barely sixteen years old, and Ross was eighteen months younger. He did not know why they were chosen. Could it be their height? They were both over six feet tall, and muscular.

Mr. Reynolds spoke with them before introducing them to their new supervisor. "You know you're different. I can't discuss the agreement with your other master," he said, referring to their grandfather. He looked at Zeek, then back at Ross. "I don't think I am breaking any promise I made by allowing you to join the survey." That ended the discussion.

When they arrived in Natchez, they received a set of clothes. They also given some new boots. The boots were of the finest leather the boys had ever seen. They slipped on without needing laces. The boys spent the four days' travel trying on the clothes and getting used to the new boots.

Being on the boat was a new experience. They enjoyed watching the water rushing along the sides of the boat. They also were fascinated by how fast the tugboat was able to push them upstream. Zeek and Ross were beginning to understand more about the world, but they still didn't know how to deal with the changes in their lives.

"Ross, we get to stay together." Zeek had overheard Mr. Reynolds say that to their new boss.

"Zeek, I think I am going to like what we will be doing," Ross commented. "It's going to be different." Ross smiled for the first time on that trip.

Zeek thought back to how Ross had stared at the floor in the hotel lobby just before their grandfather left them with Mr. Reynolds.

The time spent at the Reynolds Plantation had not been as miserable as the last few years with their mother. The only thing they knew was they were always the center of constant complaining from someone. They did not understand the reason they had to leave the Matthews Plantation.

Zeek picked up on Ross's comment about liking their new adventure. "How can we know we're going to like something when we don't even know what it is?"

They continued talking as they walked toward the men standing in line in front of a desk. When Zeek approached the desk, the man with the paperwork looked up, startled. It was obvious he saw a difference in Zeek and Ross's appearance from the slaves in front of them—slaves he had already finished paperwork for. After staring for a minute, he began reading to them that they were contracted with the survey crew, and were expected to follow the engineer's instructions and to abide by all the rules of the survey during the course of their employment. He went on to recite that they were the property of the Reynolds Plantation, and would be returned to the plantation at the end of the survey.

When he finished reading, he looked up.

"Are you Zeek?"

"Yes."

The man turned the paperwork around on the desk. He pointed to the signature line and handed Zeek a pencil.

Zeek attempted to write his name. His scribbles were actually legible.

Ross went through the same process. When the paper was turned around, he took it into his hands, like he was reading it before signing. Then he placed it back on the desk and carefully marked an 'X' for his signature.

The paperwork was finished.

Now they stood face to face with four young people who stood out from the rest. The tallest of the four stuck out his hand.

"I'm Jim Campbell," he said, shaking hands with Zeek.

"I'm Zeek," was the reply. When his eyes met

Jim Campbell's, he saw friendship.

Ross walked past them. Another young man followed him until he stopped. When Ross stopped, another one of the men stuck out his hand, saying, "I'm Ethan Massey."

Zeek and Ross helped to set up all the tents and were expecting to spend the night with the other slaves. They were surprised and excited when they were invited into the tent with Jim Campbell, Noah Sitton, Ethan Massey, and a young man named Rhodes. Zeek could not remember his first name.

The next day they all moved equipment from the dock to a ferryboat. They finished loading the equipment and thought they were ready to cross the Mississippi River, when they were told to load the mules. The mules had been brought from another plantation in northern Mississippi. They were nothing more than farm mules used to cultivate crops. Now they were going to be pack mules for the survey.

It had been interesting trying to load those mules onto the ferry. Ross and Zeek watched at first, since neither one knew anything about handling mules. The other slaves began trying to load the mules. The mules began braying, biting, and kicking to avoid getting on the ferry.

Jim Campbell and Ethan Massey joined in to help. Eventually, Ross and Zeek grabbed the mules' halters and manes, trying to get them to move forward and on the ferry boat. It had been quite a struggle.

"Zeek, it's a good thing we got all of our equipment on and fastened down before we tried loading those mules!" Jim Campbell commented.

Zeek nodded. He had quickly gotten used to working with his new friend. The four white boys from Wayne County, Tennessee, treated him differently than any other group of white men he had ever been around. Everybody had always been quick to let them know their position was one of slavery.

"Ross, you reckon they don't know we're slaves?" Zeek asked. They had never been treated as equals before. It was definitely a new experience.

"I don't know if they do or not," Ross answered. "I like all of them, especially Ethan."

Zeek often thought about who he and Ross were, starting as children on a plantation. Their lives had now turned in another direction. He decided he was going to like this new adventure just as Ross had said.

The ferry ride had been smoother than expected. A man had been sent upriver to make sure there was no barge traffic or logs headed down the river. Another man had been sent downriver to make sure they were not going to collide with a tugboat on its way up. After they each blew a horn, signaling it was all clear, the ferryboat started across the river.

They made camp on the west side of the Mississippi River. They looked back toward

Memphis as the sun began to set behind them. The shadows of the trees on the water rippled with the waves.

They had landed on a sandy dome left by the last floodwaters. When they started to unload, the loose sand had been hard to walk through. And it was difficult, as usual, to handle the mules in the loose sand.

It was now time to set up camp. The sand felt comfortable when they bedded down for the night. It felt good, and the survey crew rested for the night after a hard day.

## CHAPTER 8

After the mules had awakened everybody, they began organizing for their trip into the swamp on the west side of the Mississippi River. They would begin the survey as soon as they had their tools and equipment ready to start.

The engineer dumped tools on a canvas to be sorted and identified for use. Jim Campbell and Ethan Massey watched as Zeek and Ross organized the tools.

"You have worked with tools before," said Jim as he watched Zeek clean the edge of a new ax.

"It's what we did at the plantation," Zeek answered. "We learned how to take care of a lot of different tools."

After finishing cleaning the tools dumped on the canvas, they began unpacking all the new tools that had been shipped in wooden crates. There also were older tools in barrels that had been shipped without having been sharpened or cleaned. They cleaned and sharpened all of those, too.

Zeek and Ross continued sorting and organizing the tools by their use. The engineer stopped by a couple of times to check their progress. He watched them work.

"Jim, you take this one as your partner," he said, referring to Zeek.

He turned to Ethan and paused.

"I forgot your name," he said as he reached and touched Ethan on the shoulder. "Your partner is Ross." He pointed at Ross, then bent to more closely inspect the newly sharpened tools.

Satisfied with the way they had laid out the tools, and the work they had done to clean, repair, and sharpen the old tools, he started to walk away. As an afterthought, he turned and said, "You guys will all work together when we start moving into the woods."

~ ~ ~ ~

It had been over a week since the day the engineer had inspected the tools and equipment. They were now moving into the swamp land of Arkansas. It was difficult in the overgrown swamp and forest. After establishing the coordinates of where they were with the compass and transit, they began the survey into Arkansas.

The four men from Wayne County, Tennessee, became friends with Zeek and Ross. While Jim Campbell worked with Zeek, Ross became the assistant for Ethan Massey and Andy Rhodes. Noah Sitton's job was to coordinate all the work from where the engineer would set up the transit to where Jim and Zeek trimmed the brush. The brush had to be cleared to be able to shoot the line of the survey.

Ethan Massey and Andy Rhodes measured distance with the survey chain. A length of chain for surveying was twenty-two yards long, and had to be held as straight and level as possible before marking the distance.

It was a slow and tedious process between trimming the brush and the point when Noah would set the survey pole so the chain could be stretched and the distance measured. They headed due west, establishing a baseline for the survey of Arkansas.

They finally reached a point where the engineer set up his transit and determined the corner that was the actual starting point for the entire survey of Arkansas. It was about the tenth day when the engineer was satisfied with all of the coordinates.

"Cut a cypress limb and drive it as deep as possible here." The engineer pointed to a spot where he wanted the limb driven into the ground. After that was done, he sat down and cut letters and numbers into the side of the stake. The numbers were the distance west meridian, and the distance north latitude of the location.

"This is the beginning of the survey of the Louisiana Purchase," he declared, pointing to the ground where the stake was. Then he measured the distance to each of the larger trees around it.

"We will mark all of these trees with the coordinates from the spot where we drove the post, marking the beginning corner of the survey," he added.

They cut large flat spots on the sides of the trees, big enough to accommodate the markings the surveyor would carve into the wood. After the marking for the corner was finished, he set up the transit and began shooting the line for the beginning of the survey.

Jim and Zeek went ahead, trimming brush with two machetes. Each of them had an ax for trimming the bigger limbs. They cleaned the line of sight. It was hard work.

"You think we can get used to doing this?" Jim asked Zeek.

"I like doing this," Zeek answered. He chopped limbs from a holly bush that the surveyor had pointed toward.

As the line was being surveyed, a crew blazed a mark on the sides of the trees on each side of the line to indicate the survey had passed between the trees.

The day's work progressed. Andy Rhodes and Ethan Massey carried the chain and marked the distance. Noah was responsible for placing the survey range pole where the engineer instructed. Jim and Zeek constantly looked back to line up the trimming with the pole and the transit.

Zeek and Ross were busy with their work. They did not discuss anything about their past. They did not reminisce about their beginnings at the Matthews Plantation, nor the time they spent growing up after they had been sold by their grandfather.

They liked their new work. They liked being treated as respectfully as their new friends from Wayne County, Tennessee, were treating them.

During their conversations with their new friends, Ethan discovered that the two boys had been prevented from learning to read and write.

"I can read quite a bit," Zeek had said. It was an exaggeration. As they further discussed it, Zeek admitted, "Our mother wanted to teach us, but she was afraid."

Zeek and Ross never told their new friends who they really were. Although it was obvious they were not fully colored, they never mentioned their daddy was the plantation owner's son. They were not trying to forget, they just didn't have any idea what it might mean to the other men, and they did not want to damage their relationship with the survey crew.

The survey of the baseline had gone far enough west, and had established enough township corners to begin the survey north. Another crew started surveying south with those townships beginning at the same baseline. Crews were dropped off to start the north-to-south township lines at several points along the baseline. Zeek and Ross, along with their friends from Wayne County, Tennessee, finally turned north to survey a range line.

They had been surveying for several months before they arrived on a mountain top which was different from the others. Ethan Massey insisted they establish a base camp here. It was a large area of flat land, and had a spring practically in the middle of it. Ethan named it Big Flat. They returned each day from the survey and spent each night in the camp. It was a great location. There was no swamp, there were very few mosquitos, and they had fresh, clean water.

Jim and Zeek had become good enough at clearing the line of sight that they could work several hours ahead of the transit. They used the side trees as a line of sight to guide their way from where the transit was going to be. Sometimes they packed enough food and gear to camp and avoid the walk back and forth to the base camp every day.

They became great friends. Zeek learned about Jim's world in Wayne County, Tennessee, and finally told Jim about his own life. It did not affect their friendship at all when Jim heard Zeek's story.

One day, they trimmed the brush until it was almost dark. They had gotten more supplies from the wagon earlier in the day and were about to set up camp for the night.

"You hear that?" Zeek asked.

"Did I hear what?"

"That noise. I heard the same noise yesterday." Zeek pointed in the direction of the woods, just above where they stood in the survey path they had trimmed.

"It came from over there," Zeek said. He pointed and started walking in that direction. Jim followed.

They stood in the darkening twilight, staring into the woods. Something moved. Two faces peered at them from the brush. Two young indigenous girls cautiously stepped out. Zeek stepped forward, motioning with both hands for them to come closer.

Who were they? How did they come to be there?

# CHAPTER 9

The girls had shown up three days in a row. Jim and Zeek looked forward to seeing them again. Zeek wondered if they hid out all day, watching them. It was getting late in the fall, and with the leaves falling it was easier to see through the brush.

Jim and Zeek discussed them continuously. They felt they were beginning to be able to communicate better.

"They like you, Zeek," Jim had commented after the second day.

"I don't know how we would know," Zeek replied. "I don't think we share one word in common," he said, referring to the language barrier. He tried every gesture he knew, trying to communicate, while Jim stood and watched.

Zeek had compared skin colors with the two girls. He held out his arm alongside theirs. He pointed to his hair, and said "hair" several times. The second day he held hands with one of the girls, his favorite. He linked his fingers through hers. Jim had teased him as they walked back to camp.

"I don't think you're trying to learn a language," Jim laughed. "You're just trying to flirt."

Zeek didn't answer. He just smiled and kept walking.

"You may never get to talk to her," Jim commented, "but I believe she's going to be your woman."

Zeek didn't answer that comment, either. But he thought about how Jim had picked out the other girl and stood by her while he tried to learn some means of communication.

Neither Jim nor Zeek could remember whose idea it was to take the girls and leave the survey crew. They left camp the fourth morning with all of their belongings.

Jim had always carried a rifle and ammunition with him while they worked cutting brush. He usually killed a deer once a week for camp meat. When they decided to leave, he had the gun, along with a lot of ammunition he had stuffed into the tool bag.

The day before, Zeek spent several minutes trying to get the girls to understand that they would go with them into the woods the next day. "We are going with you," Zeek said as he pointed to himself and Jim. He spread his arms and pointed to the girls before making a motion that they were all going into the woods together.

"I believe they understood," he told Jim as they walked away planning to leave the survey the next day with the girls.

The first two nights they stayed under a bluff in places where the girls led them. They moved camp each morning. Their communication got better as the days progressed.

"Vida," Zeek's friend repeated several times before he realized she was saying her name.

"Vida, Vida," She said before hugging him and saying, "Zeek, Zeek."

Zeek did not remember how Jim and Eda had gotten together.

They arrived at a special spot along the trail. To the south there was a bluff some ten feet high. At a gap in the bluff, there was a spring bubbling up from underneath. Jim stopped. He looked around. There was a gentle sloping area with the water flowing steadily through the center of it before the stream descended down a series of ledges and joined a larger stream. There was a flat area above the bluff with an open grassy area. Looking across the creek to the west, there were large oak trees without any brush underneath, indicating the soil was deep and rich. Jim stepped across the stream, looking back toward the bluff where the water began to flow.

"Zeek, there is room enough on each side of this stream to build a cabin." He paused, then walked toward the bluff.

He pointed back toward Zeek and the two maidens. "You and Vida can build your cabin there," he said, pointing to the west side of where the water was flowing. "We will build ours here," he said as he walked back to a spot just above where Zeek and Vida stood.

This was the first time Jim or Zeek claimed either of the girls.

Their communication improved to the point where they were able to talk and plan. The two girls understood they were starting new lives with Jim and Zeek. Their marriages began as they started building their cabins.

They all worked hard. The women were good workers. The land provided for them. Jim met up with a fur trader by accident while he was hunting. They began trapping, and were successful enough to buy their clothes and supplies during the first winter.

"Zeek," Vida called from the porch of the cabin two years after. She motioned for him to come. He followed her inside and found that she had learned to cook with the new pot that he had gotten from the fur trader. He followed her to the fireplace where the pot hung over the fire. She used a piece of cloth to shield the heat from her hand while she lifted the lid and pointed to the pot.

"Johnny cake," she said as he peered into the

pot. "Just like you make," she added.

Zeek lifted the pot off the hook and set it in the middle of the table. He had made the table the first winter immediately after they got the roof on the cabin. He removed the Johnny cake from the pot and began to sample it.

"It's good," he said, looking at Vida.

Their little girl, who was barely two years old, woke up and came walking into the room. They also had a baby boy who was awake and crying.

It had been almost three years since Jim and Zeek had left the survey crew. Zeek sat on a rock below their cabins. He looked back toward the direction they had come almost three years earlier. Now they both had families and were living in the woods of Arkansas.

Zeek had no idea where they were, but he was happy. He had respect for himself and his new wife. They could not communicate well in the beginning, but he had learned enough of her language to be able to teach her his. He became the interpreter for Jim and Eda as they also learned their languages.

Zeek was proud that he was the one who had been able to teach their language to their wives, and a little bit of his wife's language to himself and Jim. Jim Campbell hadn't shown any interest in learning the indigenous language. He just loved the fact that they had found the girls and saved them from whatever might have happened to them living in the woods.

Zeek had not shared any of his history with Vida He had learned from her that she was part of a tribe that came south every year in mid-summer to spend a few months under the bluffs in northern Arkansas. When they arrived the year they met Jim and Zeek, their tribe found that the place where they had planned to stay had been taken over by another tribe.

Zeek was never able to get many details about the battle between the two small groups. He just knew that the two girls had run into the woods and could not find their way back to their tribe. She couldn't really tell him how long they'd been hiding when they heard Zeek and Jim trimming brush.

"We were just glad to see bodies," was Vida's description of when they saw Zeek and Jim.

The time had been good for all of them. The women felt secure with their men. Zeek wondered how his wife looked at him. He was never sure of his identity. If you went by skin color, he was barely darker than Jim Campbell. Vida was a different color. Her skin showed more of the copper red of her people than Zeek had seen in most of the northern tribes.

Their children were throwbacks. They looked more like Zeek's grandfather who had sold him to a fellow plantation owner years before in New Orleans.

Race didn't seem to matter to the people living in those cabins below a bluff, cabins where a spring flowed out between them. They were building a life together, and growing as a family.

# CHAPTER 10

Zeek was at peace and comfortable with his new life. He liked living with his wife and children in the cabin next door to Jim Campbell. He was happy and content. Jim, however, still feared for Zeek's freedom, and lived cautiously, wondering when and if it could become a problem.

They had gotten to where they would venture out and leave the cabin. They started off to the trading post which had been built at the mouth of Seiler's Creek.

Zeek was some twenty paces in front of Jim as they followed the trail above the ledge, heading east, away from the cabins. The trail meandered in and out of the cedars just above where the bluff dropped off into the hollow. It obviously had been a game trail before people began using it. It had become a passage between the cabins and the trading post.

Zeek looked at the trail. The path was a combination of black soil with a few rocks mixed in with some sand. There was very little grass growing below the trail. Water flowing down the hill had cut little trenches across the path. The water followed these little ditches until it fell over the bluff. The trail followed the edge of the bluff, and turned sharply at each little hollow where it intersected with the bluff line. The trail descended down into the hollow, crossing what usually was a dry streambed, before it ascended back up to the ledge.

Zeek's mind went back to the survey. He hated when the line would run continuously along the edge of a bluff. They had been trying to survey somewhere to the north and east of where their cabins were now located when Andy Rhodes fell off the bluff. Jim and Zeek had been in the hollow below where Andy fell. They were waiting for the engineer to appear before they tried to establish the line into the hollow.

They did not hear Andy Rhodes scream when he fell. They did not know what the noise from the survey crew was about. They continued trying to find an open spot where they could see the point where the survey line would descend from the bluff.

They joined the search for Andy after they learned what had happened. Andy was one of the four boys from Wayne County, Tennessee, who treated Zeek and Ross very well. They joined one of the search groups, but were not with the people who found Andy's body.

Zeek's thoughts returned to the trail he and Jim were following.

"What's that?" Zeek pointed to something laying across the path some thirty yards in front of him. He turned to Jim.

Jim whispered, "It's a body." He reached for Zeek's shoulder and continued to whisper. "Let's go into the woods and watch to see if anyone else is around."

They left the trail and split up. Zeek went up the hill above the trail about fifty yards in front of the body. He stopped where he could see it. Jim did the same thing about the same distance in the opposite direction.

Zeek had no idea how long it had been. He had not heard any sounds during the time he waited. Nor had he seen any movement. He heard a whistle, and then Jim said, "Meet me on the trail," barely loud enough for Zeek to hear.

They spent over an hour examining the body. It was a black man. He was not a mixed color like Zeek. He was obviously a slave. The back of his skull had been bashed in. Zeek and Jim both wondered what reason anyone would have to do this and leave him lying in the trail.

They went through the pockets of his clothes. Jim discovered a paper inside the vest pocket. He studied it for a minute, then read aloud. "This paper confirms that Noel Milam has received his freedom and is a man in his own right subject to live free." The paper was notarized and was signed by a plantation owner in Tennessee. The back of the paper indicated the page and the book where it was recorded at a courthouse. Jim determined it was a valid document.

Jim read the description on the paper of the height and weight of Noel Milam. "You're about the same size as this fellow," he said.

Zeek didn't say anything. He gave no thought to the size of the man on the paper. Jim had read it, but it did not carry any meaning to Zeek at the time.

They spent the rest of the afternoon burying the man. They returned to their cabins and retrieved the tools for digging a grave. They did not tell their wives or children what they were doing. They returned and moved the body up the hill above the cedar glade. After they dug a grave, Jim and Zeek lined the bottom with cedar cuttings. Then they placed the man into the grave, and covered the body with a lot more of the cedar limbs. They hoped it would protect the body from the dirt they shoveled to cover the cedar limbs.

They found two large stones to cover the top of the grave. They then went around the perimeter with other stones until they had stacked them in a dome over the grave. They did not try to put up a marker.

As they left the grave, Jim said, "Zeek, you're a free man. You are Noel Milam."

Zeek was oblivious to what he meant. He had never pretended to be anybody but Zeek.

They returned to the cabin, what they had originally left to do totally forgotten. They had been on their way heading to the trading post, and to check to see if the beavers had rebuilt one of their dams—the dam where a spring dumped its water into Seiler's Creek. The creek flowed about fifty yards in front of their cabins.

Zeek did not mention what had happened. Nor did Jim, until a few days later when he asked Zeek to come over. Zeek came and sat down on the porch with Jim, and waited for Jim to start the discussion.

## CHAPTER 11

Zeek greeted Jim and sat down in front of him, facing away, with his legs hanging over the side of the porch. His mind raced. He wondered why Jim needed to talk. They usually had their discussions while they worked. It was unusual for Jim to ask him to come over to the porch.

Jim held the paper in his hand that he had removed from the dead man.

Zeek turned and leaned back against a porch post. He raised his left foot up, setting it on the porch while his right leg continued to dangle.

"What've you got on your mind?" Zeek asked as he stared at the paper in Jim's hand.

Jim stood up, walked over to Zeek and handed the paper and envelope to him. He turned and went back to sit down before he answered Zeek's question.

"I don't know for sure," Jim said. His voice had the sound of a lingering question.

"You don't know what for sure?"

"I told you the other day after I read that paper, ' Zeek, you can be a free man.' I said you could be Noel Milam."

Zeek did not say anything. He handed the paper and envelope back to Jim. He did not bother to open the envelope or look at the paper. He was confused by the suggestion. The only name he had ever known was Zeek. When he thought of a last name he always thought of being a Matthews. He had been born on a plantation by that name, and his father was Caleb Matthews. He would never feel comfortable changing his name.

"Why would I need to do that?" he asked.

"I don't know that you need to change your name," Jim answered, "but there may come a day when someone will come looking for us."

Jim spent the next few minutes trying to explain his fears to Zeek.

"Zeek, I don't even know where we are. Searcy County, I think," Jim said, trying to start the conversation about what he considered a predicament. "We could both be in jeopardy for having deserted the survey." He expressed the fear he had of someone reporting them.

Jim could see the concerned expression that came over Zeek's face when he mentioned the fear of being in violation of some law.

"I don't know if there's any law enforcement anywhere close to us," he continued, thinking about how few people there were in the area.

"When I go to Leslie for supplies I hear a lot of talk about Arkansas becoming a territory," Jim said. "I understand now we have a territorial governor."

Jim also began to explain the other things he worried about.

"We have never filed any paperwork on this land." Jim stood up, continuing to explain that they could not even file until they had a description of where they were. He knew Ethan Massey had the fieldnotes and also had logged them onto a map each night after they had finished that day's survey.

"We need Ethan to return to Arkansas," he said, looking across the creek.

Jim walked to the end of the porch and pointed west. "There is too much good land there for people not to settle," he said. "That land is very fertile."

The land, for the most part, was covered by huge oak trees with little or no underbrush. There was grass growing in the open areas and underneath the trees. The soil was black and fertile, just like the area around the trading post at Leslie.

"We'll have to have our paperwork done before people come to settle, or they can lay claim to our property," he said. "And they will come."

Jim sat back down. "As more people come, there will be law enforcement," Jim said. "I've been hoping Ethan and Noah would return. Of course, they will want to settle at Big Flat." Jim referred to the area where the base camp had been. The survey crew had all enjoyed the time around the spring with fresh water and no mosquitos.

Zeek wondered what all this had to do with his name. Or the letter they'd found on the dead man.

He thought back over the last few years. They had built two cabins. They had wives. He was happy. He had never had any plans for his life until after they left the survey crew with the girls and built the cabins.

Zeek was not anxious for anything to change. He had been responsible for the farming and taking care of their livestock, which now included several pigs and cows. Vida and Eda were asking for chickens. They could hear the roosters crowing from the farms down the hollow. After they investigated the noise, they wanted some chickens of their own.

Zeek had made a deal for some of the next batch. He spent several hours visiting with their new neighbors and looking over the chicken coop. They also had built a wire cage around the chickens. When he learned about how much trouble it was, he began to wonder if he wanted any chickens.

Zeek's mind had wandered away from his and Jim's discussion.

"Why do you think I need to do this?" he asked, getting back on track.

Jim looked at Zeek, sitting on the edge of the porch. He thought that at a glance you couldn't possibly see that Zeek was a black man. As he had gotten older, he had become more angular in stature, and also square-jawed. He had more of an Irish look. His hair was not of the same texture as the man they buried. While it wasn't straight, it had just enough curl to accent his face.

"When somebody comes asking who you are, you could give them the paper, and maybe they would be satisfied," Jim answered after some thought.

Jim stood up. He took the paper and returned it to the place where it had been stored above the porch post Zeek was leaning against.

"We will just leave the paper where it is," Jim said as he sat back down.

"Jim, I don't know what to do about any of this," Zeek added. "I was born at the Matthews Plantation and I lived with Missy, who was my mom. I never knew there was anything different about me and Ross. We had a daddy. I remember him, but he went away. It was never explained to us."

Zeek got up from the porch and started to walk away. He turned back and bent over, placing both hands palm down on the floor of the porch. He looked up at Jim Campbell and finished what he had to say.

"I trust you," he said, looking up at Jim. "I know you're the best friend I've ever had, and I'll do whatever you say I need to do." He paused. "But I don't want to change my name."

Jim watched as Zeek walked toward the lot where they kept the milk cows. He thought of Zeek's determination to take care of his family. He thought of how he never had any control over who he was until after they left the survey crew.

Zeek watched the cows as they munched some hay. It was almost milking time. He went back to the cabin and got the milk pail. He started his evening chores.

There had been no decision about the paper, just a discussion. Zeek would have to give it a lot more thought before he would take the paper from the top of the post and claim he was anybody but Zeek.

## CHAPTER 12

Zeek was working in the garden when he heard a fox horn blow three times, really sharply. The horn was a hollowed-out bull's horn with a cedar mouthpiece. Jim had designed it to where it was easy to blow and gave out a sound that could be heard throughout the valley.

They taught their wives how to blow the horn. Three sharp blasts meant there were visitors. It had only been necessary to blow the horn a few times since they had been living in the cabins. Zeek didn't immediately run to the house. He finished digging around the vegetable plant. He put his hoe over his shoulder and began walking toward the sound of the horn.

He heard voices when he got closer. Jim was greeting Ethan Massey and Noah Sitton from the survey crew. He recognized both of them. He walked closer, not knowing what to expect. He stopped a few paces from them. Jim introduced him as "Noel Milam."

Zeek was shocked at the introduction. While he had listened to Jim about the paper they had found on the dead man, he knew he had not agreed to take his identity.

Jim Campbell continued with the story. He explained to Noah and Ethan how Zeek could take the identity of Noel Milam and become a free man. Zeek could not understand why Jim felt an urge to explain this during the first few minutes of visiting with their friends from the survey. He wondered why.

Ethan and Noah both knew he was a slave contracted to the survey crew. Zeek knew they knew him as Zeek.

He started to interrupt Jim and tell them he wasn't going to use that paper. But he had too much respect for Jim Campbell to do that.

Zeek listened. He watched the expression on Noah's face as he listened to Jim's explanation. Jim was intent on explaining to Ethan how the paper was going to give Zeek his freedom.

Zeek didn't know how he felt when Jim went ahead and invited everybody that had come from Wayne County, Tennessee, to settle in the valley. He heard there were nineteen wagons. He tried to visualize how many people there would be with those wagons. He glanced at his porch where Vida and his children stood listening to the conversation. He wondered what Vida thought when she heard their life might change dramatically when they added all the new neighbors.

He watched as Noah and Ethan rode away.

After they had gotten some distance from Jim and Zeek, Jim explained about his comments.

"I wanted them to know I consider you a free man. If they had any idea of turning you back over as a slave, they could forget it."

"I understand," Zeek said.

Several months after the conversation between the four old friends, Ethan Massey led the members of his family and their friends into the valley. They settled close by. They decided to name the community Campbell, after Jim Campbell, because he had settled there first with Zeek and their wives.

They all worked together to get their cabins built for the newcomers to the valley. Zeek helped. He chinked the cracks between the logs on Ethan's cabin. It was built about a hundred yards across the creek and west from Jim's and Zeek's cabins.

There was a lot of discussion about the land. Ethan had a map, which had gotten wet somewhere between Tennessee and Arkansas. However, he also had a copy of the logbook with the survey notes for the area. They were able to recreate the map.

Ethan and Jim took the map and the notes to the

land office, located somewhere north of the Buffalo River. They came back with patents and deeds registered to all the families in the valley.

Zeek stood wondering if Jim had anything for him. After everyone left, Jim walked over and put his hand on Zeek's shoulder.

"I didn't try to register or patent a deed for you, Zeek." Jim looked away toward the cabin being finished for Ethan. "I was afraid it would cause a problem," he added. "I could see you didn't like it when I tried to explain the Noel Milam paper."

Jim stood with a look of compassion for his good friend Zeek. He went on to say, "I don't believe Noah and Ethan are concerned about your identity."

He started to walk away, then stopped and added, "You don't have to worry about land. I filed on enough for both of us, and if I've got anything, you will always have your part."

The activity in the valley increased dramatically with the new settlers working to develop their homesteads. The fur-bearing animals were harvested at a very fast rate. The fur trader said, "I'm buying more furs than ever before, but it's not going to last very much longer. We've about got all of them."

Almost two years later, everybody was settled into their new homes. Zeek liked having neighbors and got along well with everyone. Zeek's family was accepted without any questions about his wife being indigenous, nor had there been any mention of his race. No one seemed to realize that he was one quarter Choctaw, one quarter black, and with a white father. They had no way of knowing his dad was the son of a plantation owner.

There were a large number of children in the valley. They were getting along, and were proud of their community. No one ever knew whose idea it was to build a school. They just agreed to build the building. Ethan took the lead.

Earl Massey, Ethan's dad, decided they needed their own trading post. When they finished the trading post they named it "Campbell's Trade Stop."

Zeek and his family got along well because of their ability to contribute to their neighbors. He was the best craftsman among the men. Whether it was building the school or the trading post, everyone wanted to work with Zeek.

## CHAPTER 13

The blast of the fox horn could be heard throughout the Campbell community. When Zeek heard the horn, he was repairing the fence around the upper garden. The garden was named the upper garden because it was above the cabins on a ledge with sandy soil. The garden was special because they grew the smooth-skinned sweet potatoes and great-tasting squash in the light-colored soil. Jim and Zeek's families had shared the garden ever since they settled years earlier.

He was startled to hear the three sharp blasts. It meant there was a stranger coming toward the cabins.

Zeek started toward the cabin. He could not remember the last time when the horn had been blown. Probably when Ethan and Noah had arrived. He remembered that because it was the first time Vida had ever blown it. He wondered if she had blown it this time. It had to be a stranger because she knew everybody in the community.

He grew more concerned as he walked down the hill. When he came through the gap in the ledge, he could see Jim Campbell. He wondered why Jim faced the ledge. He quickly had the answer. The two men Jim was talking to had their backs to Zeek. He knew Jim had deliberately positioned himself where he would be able to see Zeek as he came toward the cabin. Neither one of the men talking with him realized that when Jim raised his arm high above his head and brought it down slowly, that it was a signal for Zeek not to come any closer, to stay away.

Zeek went to the corn crib and began shelling corn. He knew Jim would come and find him.

"Well, Zeek…" he said slowly, "…those men came looking for you."

"For me?"

"Yes. You, Zeek," Jim answered emotionally.

"What kind of questions?" Zeek asked.

"Not questions, Zeek. No, not questions." Jim looked down at his feet as he repeated the comment. He was trying to decide the best way to tell Zeek the two men were there to inquire about the slave who ran away from the survey crew. He finally just blurted it out.

"They know who I am?" Zeek stated it more as a fact than a question. Before Jim could comment,

Zeek continued. "They know I am here." He stated it as an absolute fact.

"They said they would be back with papers from the court to take you back to the Reynolds Plantation in Mississippi." Jim said the words he had always dreaded hearing himself.

Zeek's shoulders slumped as he heard.

They walked to the chicken lot with the corn Zeek had shelled to feed the chickens. They quietly tossed corn into the chicken lot. Their thoughts raced back in time to the day they left the survey. Zeek thought about all the years he had lived here.

His daughter and son were grown and married. He had three grandchildren. He knew everybody in the valley. He also knew a man in Leslie very well, Mr. Hayes, who owned the flour mill and the trading post. Zeek's son worked for Mr. Hayes. His daughter lived on Oxley Mountain, above Campbell.

In all the years there had been no mention of race. Jim Campbell had never told anyone other than Ethan and Noah about the Noel Milam paper. Zeek had given his children the last name Matthews. He did so without any explanation. All of the paperwork he had ever filled out was Zeek Matthews.

His skin color had never been an issue in Searcy County. It just wasn't. There all kinds of mixtures of races, with indigenous and every European settler being the most common. You could go to the trading post in Leslie and see three red-headed people with fair complexions visiting with dark-skinned people with obvious indigenous blood.

"Jim, what should I do?" Zeek finally asked after they had been standing next to the fence around the chicken pen for some time.

"Nothing," Jim answered. He didn't tell Zeek what he had told the two men. He had told them he had no idea what they were talking about. Jim was feeling guilty. He had told an absolute lie. But he was not going to turn in his children's uncle and see him taken away. Besides, he would never betray his old friend.

"We will just wait and see if we ever hear anything else about it," Jim said.

They walked away from the chicken pen. They agreed never to tell their wives, or anyone, until it became a real problem.

Jim worried that Zeek's face would tell the story to his wife. He looked sad. He wasn't good at hiding his troubles.

# CHAPTER 14

Life had never gotten back to normal for Zeek after the threat of being claimed by the Reynolds Plantation became a reality. It was now almost two years since the men had come asking about him.

The sheriff showed up with a summons for Zeek to appear at a hearing at the Searcy County Courthouse in Marshall to determine if he was a runaway slave. The plantation from Mississippi was prepared to prove that Zeek was their property. The hearing would be for them to present their proof.

Ethan Massey had become the leader of the community. He was the one everybody relied on for advice. After Zeek was served with the summons to appear in court, he gave the paperwork to Jim Campbell.

Ethan and Jim went to see Noah Sitton immediately. Ethan led the fight to avoid the hearing. Ethan went with Zeek to hire an attorney to represent them. They hired Joel Bratton, who had an office in the basement of the new courthouse. He was the best attorney available.

Jim Campbell had mentioned the paper they had taken off the dead man. It was quickly decided that under no circumstance could they use that paper.

Zeek knew Caleb Matthews was his father. He had taken Matthews as his last name. He had never explained the circumstances of his birth, and he didn't plan to try to use that as a defense.

Joel Bratton was told the entire story. He expressed doubts they had any defense. A new law had been passed through the U.S. Congress in 1850, allowing plantations to recover runaway slaves. If a slave was one quarter black, and any parent was ever the property of a plantation, their rights to ownership stayed intact.

"Noah, what difference do it make who I am, just as long as I am what I am?" Zeek asked.

Noah, except for the time he was back in Wayne County trying to figure out when he was going to move to Arkansas, had been acquainted with Zeek for over thirty years. He remembered when they met in Memphis and joined the survey crew.

"Zeek, I don't know," Noah answered, not sure if he understood the question.

"Will I have to go back?" It was a question Zeek had continuously asked ever since the men came looking for him.

Zeek sat in the corner of Joel Bratton's office in the courthouse at Marshall, Arkansas.

Joel Bratton paced the room in front of his desk. He went to the window and looked out at the crowd. He thought about what all he had read about people showing up for a hanging. This time it was for a trial to try to put a man back into slavery.

"We will not offer any defense until we've heard their entire case," Joel stated, looking at Zeek.

There was no expression on Zeek's face at all.

Joel led the way out of his office as they started up the stairs to the courtroom. Ethan Massey, Jim Campbell, and Noah Sitton followed behind him. Zeek was behind Noah, but caught up with Jim.

He whispered to Jim, "I'm not scared, I just don't know what to think." His whisper wasn't very loud, but loud enough that all the men headed into the courtroom heard him.

Nathaniel Sitton and Earl Massey had not been in Joel Bratton's office. They quickly tried to follow up the stairs. They were both in their upper seventies and had come to Arkansas following their boys from Wayne County, Tennessee. They supported everything about trying to help Zeek.

Nathaniel thought about the time when he met Zeek. He wondered why he was considered a slave. He could barely see any evidence of black blood. He had heard the stories. Earl and Nathaniel discussed how well Zeek fit into the community. Seemingly, no one had ever noticed his difference in race.

"If you just saw him for the first time, I doubt you would realize he had any black blood," Earl Massey commented to Nathaniel before they climbed the stairs to go to the hearing.

There were not enough chairs for everyone to sit with Zeek. Noah Sitton and Nathaniel went to stand by the south wall of the courtroom. Zeek sat down next to Joel Bratton, his attorney. Ethan moved a chair around where he could sit on Joel's right side. They waited for the hearing to begin.

"All rise." The standard call for the start of the hearing was said as the judge entered the room.

Zeek's eyes scanned the entire courtroom. He noticed a man dressed exactly the way he remembered the plantation owner who had picked him and his brother up in New Orleans. He also remembered that man, Mr. Reynolds, had been good to them.

Over the next few minutes the judge read the purpose of the hearing. It was to determine if a slave going by the name of Zeek was the property of a plantation in Mississippi. Zeek looked at the plantation owner. He was dressed in white. A ruffled shirt could be seen inside the lapels of his suit. And he had a huge wide-brimmed hat. He was not very tall.

Zeek thought he was just about the same size as the man who bought Zeek and his brother, Ross, from their grandfather who owned the Matthews Plantation. Zeek continued looking at the man.

"He's come to take me away from my family," Zeek whispered to himself. He feared he was about to lose the life he had built in Arkansas.

He didn't know why he was thinking of who he was. His thoughts went back to Caleb Matthews, his father. He never called him "dad" before he left the plantation. Zeek never got him before he left. Zeek was only six years old then, but he remembered Caleb being a lot taller than the plantation owner dressed in white. Zeek was just over six feet tall and he figured his dad was that tall.

While Zeek had been studying the man who was there to claim him as his property, the hearing had proceeded. Evidence of Zeek leaving the survey had been presented. They presented the contract between the plantation and the surveyor. They also presented an affidavit that when the survey was over, Zeek had not returned to them.

Zeek was not expecting what happened next.

Ross was sworn in as a witness. Zeek had not seen Ross in over thirty years. He watched as his brother was sworn in. When the court clerk asked Ross to state his name, he said, "I'm Ross," without a last name or any explanation.

After Ross was seated, the attorney made a statement that they had brought Ross, who was a slave on the Reynolds Plantation, and he would be able to identify the property in question. It bothered Zeek to be referred to simply as property.

"Can you identify the man sitting at the table?" the attorney asked Ross, as he pointed directly at Zeek.

"Yes, sir," Ross stated. He shifted in the witness chair and looked at Zeek. "That's my brother, Zeek."

Zeek and Ross had been separated when Zeek decided to go with Jim Campbell. The court did not enter into any discussion about Zeek having left the survey and taking an indigenous woman for a wife. They did not present any history beyond him leaving the survey. The two brothers stared at each other, showing no emotion.

The plantation owner was arrogant. He was there to put on a show for the crowd. He was trying to show that he was a man of power. The judge would ask him to remove his hat, and he would. Momentarily. He would then put it back on and smile at everyone in the courtroom. He even lit a cigar in defiance of the courtroom rules.

After his attorney finished presenting the evidence, he asked the judge if he was ready to make a ruling.

"If that's all the evidence you have, sir, I believe I can rule on this case," the judge stated.

Joel Bratton had not even been allowed to offer a defense. The law passed in 1852 clearly stated that plantation owners had a right to recover runaway slaves. Before he could raise an objection and ask to be able to present a defense, the plantation owner jumped to his feet and interrupted the judge.

"That man is my property!" he said, standing up and pointing his finger at Zeek. He then turned, waving his hat and addressing the crowd. "I'm taking him back to Mississippi and he's going to work twice as hard to pay me back for the time I've lost!" He was enjoying making this statement.

The judge, irritated at the outburst, posed a question. "What is the value you place on your property, sir?"

The plantation owner turned and faced the judge before he said, "He's worth $1700 and not a dime less."

Before the judge could respond, Mr. Hayes stood up and asked to be heard. The judge granted him permission to speak.

"You will sell him to me today for $1700?" Mr. Hayes said, more of a statement than a question. He owned the flour mill in Leslie and a hardware store, plus he was the largest farmer in the county. He never mentioned that Zeek's son was one of his best employees.

When the plantation owner nodded and agreed he would take $1700, Mr. Hayes asked the judge to hold the hearing. "I will be right back."

Zeek was not sure what he had just heard. He whispered to Joel, his attorney, "Can they just sell me?"

Joel began trying to explain to Zeek that as property of the plantation owner, yes, he could be sold. Before he could finish, they heard someone running up the steps.

The crowd was silent, listening intently. Mr. Hayes, along with two boys who worked with him, re-entered the courtroom. All eyes followed him as he approached the judge's bench. When he got there, he turned and asked the plantation owner to join him.

"You said $1700 and he would be mine," Mr. Hayes stated. When the plantation owner nodded his head, Mr. Hayes started counting the money and laying it on the front of the judge's bench. As he counted each hundred-dollar bill, the crowd leaned forward toward the front of the courtroom. He counted out $1700. All eyes were on the money. And then he continued counting $300 more.

"I am giving you $300 extra," he said. Mr. Hayes handed $2000 to the plantation owner. "The extra $300 is to cover your expenses to get out of Arkansas, and you're not to ever come back."

Zeek sat quietly, and watched as Mr. Hayes summoned Joel Bratton to the bench in front of the judge.

"Make out a bill of sale to this man," Mr. Hayes said to Joel as he pointed to the plantation owner. And after he signs it, make out a legal paper that says Zeek Matthews is a free man and no longer the property of anyone."

There was a hush in the courtroom. It took a few seconds for the crowd to understand what had just happened. Then there was a burst of applause louder than any ever heard before in an Arkansas courtroom.

Zeek never got a chance to offer his thanks to Mr. Hayes. Too many people were shaking his hand and giving him hugs, congratulating him on his freedom.

All the people who went to the hearing with Zeek left the courtroom. Zeek rode home in the buggy with Ethan and Earl Massey. Jim Campbell followed on his horse. Noah and Nathaniel Sitton rode home in their buggy. They were not sure what they had witnessed, nor did they understand.

"Son," commented Nathaniel to Noah, "this is not the end of the slavery question."

# CHAPTER 15

Caleb Matthews turned the closed sign around to show the office was open. He picked up the newspaper from the shop before he opened the door and went inside.

The sign above the door read, "Caleb Matthews, Attorney at Law." Caleb's law practice had gone well, and he made a decent living. He had worked out of that office for over twenty-five years. It was located a few blocks from Independence Hall in Philadelphia, Pennsylvania. He moved there after finishing law school in New York.

Caleb married the girl he met at Dartmouth, from St. Louis, and they had been happy. Caleb had never told his wife about Zeek and Ross.

He visited the plantation in Alabama once every five years. He had not enjoyed going back to the plantation. When he made his first trip back to Alabama, he had agreed with his mother that the boys would be a family secret never to be revealed.

During one of those visits he was in the presence of Missy for a short period of time. The nerves he felt, and the guilt while he was in her presence disturbed him very much. It was several years before he made a return visit.

Caleb unrolled *The Philadelphia Enquirer* on his desk. He began glancing at the headlines. As he scrolled through the paper, something caught his eye. It was a story of a trial in a small town in Arkansas. It involved the ownership of a slave.

His attention was drawn to the line, "plantation owner sells slave before judge can render a verdict."

The story went on to say a slave by the name of Zeek Matthews was the subject of the court hearing. Zeek had disappeared in late 1817 while he was a member of a survey crew.

Caleb read it in disbelief.

The story gave details of the life of the slave, including the fact that he had been bought in New Orleans. And then it expressed the amazement at the number of people who showed up to support the slave at the hearing, especially since he had been living as a free man and was a respected member of the Campbell community.

Caleb continued reading. He read that one of the witnesses for the plantation owner was the brother of the runaway slave. The judge was going to render a verdict without allowing a defense after Ross, the slave's brother, identified him.

Caleb stared at the newspaper. He read the article three times before he was fully convinced.

"It's the boys," he declared, as he laid the paper down on his desk.

He decided to go to Arkansas. He decided it was time to tell his wife the whole story, and why he had to go to Arkansas. He gave no thought to the consequences.

Caleb sat down in the seat of the train, waiting for it to leave the station.

"I don't think she believed any of it," he said to himself.

His ticket said he would arrive in West Plains, Missouri, on Tuesday. That would make it a two-day trip. He would ride the train through St. Louis, but he didn't plan to stop. He was not making this trip to visit his two sons in college, he was going to Arkansas to see Zeek.

Caleb asked for the best horse available at the livery stable when he rented the buggy in West Plains. The man who rented him the horse told him the best way to go to Arkansas was to go south and cross the White River at Cotter.

When Caleb asked for additional information about getting to Marshall, Arkansas, the man said, "They are building a railroad from Memphis to Springfield, Missouri, and I think you can get directions to Marshall, Arkansas, when you get to Cotter."

Without admitting that he had no idea where Marshall actually was, he knew that Cotter would be close enough for them to give Caleb the directions he needed. The man went on to explain that Marshall was the county seat of Searcy County.

Caleb remembered that, according to the newspaper story, Searcy County Circuit Court was where the trial was held.

Caleb spent the night in a hotel at Cotter. The hotel had been built to accommodate the railroad workers. He listened to the gossip at the hotel restaurant. He had told no one what his trip was about. The entire discussion in the restaurant was about a court case. Zeek's trial. Evidently it was the main topic of gossip around north Arkansas.

Caleb listened to another traveler during dinner as the man told the story. The way that man told it was that a businessman interrupted the trial and purchased the slave's freedom.

"The man who owned the slave set the price at $1700, but the businessman paid $2000. He told the owner that the extra $300 was for him to get out of Arkansas and never come back." The man, who was dining at the next table, took a drink of tea, then concluded by saying, "I'd like to see that slave. He must have some good friends around where he lives."

Caleb listened with no expression on his face. He thought how unbelievable it would sound if he told the man that the slave was his son, and that he was on his way to visit him.

Caleb was always very competent. He would walk into a courtroom full of confidence, completely ready to represent his client. But as he traveled the next morning along the road toward Campbell, Arkansas, he was nervous. By listening to the talk at dinner the previous evening, he had learned a whole community had shown up in support of the slave.

"That Zeek Matthews has *some* friends," one man commented. "I doubt anybody would pay $2000 for me under any circumstances."

When Caleb got to Marshall, he went directly to the sheriff's office. He needed better directions on how to get to the Campbell community. The sheriff looked at him. Caleb was still dressed as an attorney. He had put on some loose-fitting dungarees, but his shirt and the new boots he bought for the trip still said he was a lawyer.

The sheriff began questioning him. He wanted to know who he wanted to see at Campbell.

"Zeek Matthews," said Caleb. "I am his father." He turned to face the window.

The sheriff came out from behind his desk and got in front of Caleb.

"Let me shake your hand," he said without explaining why. He became very friendly, and offered to make the trip to Campbell with Caleb.

Caleb accepted his offer. They went to the buggy and started the trip to see Zeek.

During the buggy ride from Marshall through

the countryside, Caleb and Sheriff Kirk became friends. Caleb shared all the details he knew about the trial, and he shared his personal story of how Zeek and Ross came to be. The sheriff was amazed. He filled in details about the trial to Caleb. Caleb listened intently when the sheriff told how Zeek had lived all these years in peace. No one had ever accused him of being a runaway slave. Not until a bounty hunter showed up asking questions.

"That bounty hunter had a list of every slave who ever ran off from the plantations," Kirk said. Then he added, "When you asked me if I knew a man named Zeek...." Kirk paused before he went on to tell Caleb how he had spent several minutes bragging about what a fine man Zeek Matthews was before he realized he had just read the name "Zeek" on the list.

When the wheels of the buggy ran through water, it splashed water in the air, and Caleb almost got wet. The sheriff drove a lot faster than he normally would have. Each time they crossed a creek, the buggy wheels did the same thing. Caleb was just hanging on, trying to keep straight in his mind the turns they made.

"This is Seiler's Creek," the sheriff said as they turned and went up the creek. "This is the creek that will go to Zeek's place." He explained that the creek they had just crossed before was Long Creek. The road began alternating sides of the creek, crossing almost constantly.

Caleb sat on Zeek's front porch with the sheriff while Vida went to blow the fox horn. The horn hadn't been blown but a few times to alert Zeek before he came to the house.

After the three sharp blasts, Caleb sat nervously, awaiting Zeek's arrival.

He watched as Zeek walked into the yard below the porch. It was like a picture from the past. Zeek walked with the same pride Caleb had taught him when he was not quite five years old.

"Son, walk with your head up. Don't ever look down and act as if you are afraid."

Caleb remembered those instructions as Zeek walked toward him.

He sat still. He had told Vida he was Caleb Matthews, Zeek's dad.

Vida met Zeek in the yard, but didn't say anything before she reached him. Zeek was puzzled at the way she came and met him, then walked with him toward the man sitting on the porch.

Caleb stood up.

Zeek stopped. His mind raced as he looked at the man standing on his porch. A vision returned of a time underneath the live oak on the Matthews Plantation. He thought he recognized his dad. His mind raced back in time as he tried to make sense of what he saw.

He started to run to the porch, but then stopped and looked again. He was now sure. It was his dad. Time stood still as he covered the distance between them. Over forty years had passed since he had seen his dad.

He went up the steps of the porch and stuck out his hand toward Caleb. Caleb did not shake his hand.

Vida watched the expressions of shock on Caleb's and Zeek's faces turned to joy. With a mixture of laughter and crying, they exchanged hugs. Not a word was said as they sat down. They were too emotional to talk. They sat there with Caleb in the rocker, and Zeek on one knee holding his dad's hand, making sure this was real.

Sheriff Kirk left the porch. Vida went with him to the barn to get a horse to ride back to Marshall. When they returned, Caleb and Zeek were deep in conversation.

"Zeek, if and when your dad should leave," Sheriff Kirk said, "you can ride to Marshall with him and pick up your horse."

Zeek did not answer Sheriff Kirk, he just nodded his head as the sheriff mounted the horse and rode away.

Neither Caleb nor Zeek could remember how they got started having a conversation. They talked about their lives. They had fifty years' worth, from a survey crew to meeting a wife in the woods, having to learn to communicate, and living in the community of Campbell, of a father becoming a lawyer and having a family separate from Zeek and Ross. They listened intently as each one told about their life.

Caleb was a special guest. All the neighbors came by to meet Zeek's dad. A lot of their stories were shared, along with secrets that had been kept for a long time.

Caleb was pleased he had met his son, but soon it was time for him to go back to Philadelphia.

On the trip back to Philadelphia, Caleb was filled with thoughts of what could've been. He stopped thinking that way, realizing that they never had a choice. Caleb had become who he was, and Zeek had become who he was, including being now a free man.

Caleb never relayed much of the story to his family in Philadelphia. Nor did he ever tell his wife's family in St. Louis. He went back to practicing law in the courts of Pennsylvania, at peace with himself.

# CHAPTER 16

The afternoon shadows of October were darker and deeper than a month earlier. Where Zeek sat on the porch, the sunlight beamed brighter, while the shadows deepened. The sun continued going down, and the long shadows of the trees crept toward the porch.

Zeek sat on the original porch built with the cabin. The cabin had been extended over the years. He liked sitting in the same spot where he sat in the beginning. The door behind him opened into what had become the living room. It had a large fireplace next to the ledge at the back of the house.

Jim and Zeek had built their cabins twenty-five feet apart. After they moved in, they built a walkway connecting them together. They did not put a cover over it in the beginning, but it allowed their wives to go from cabin to cabin without ever walking on the ground. Zeek remembered when they were trying to ask for another walkway to be built. Vida would say, "Go, and again go." She pointed as she said that, but neither Zeek nor Jim understood at first. The language barrier was too strong for them to understand their wives wanted a bridge across the water from the spring. They wanted to be able to stay out of the mud and water.

"You have any idea what she wants?" Zeek had asked Jim.

"I believe I do," Jim replied. He went on to explain they wanted to be able to go out the back of the cabins and stay on a walkway while getting water and food from the spring box.

Zeek smiled as he thought back to when they finally got the bridge with steps finished. It allowed the two maidens to be able to get water from the spring without tracking mud into the cabins. They insisted on keeping a clean house. Zeek's smile grew bigger as he remembered that when they started building the cabins, Jim and Zeek had planned to have a dirt floor. Even with the language barrier, they were able to understand their wives' objections.

To this day, some thirty-five years later, they still didn't know where the girls ever saw a wooden floor.

Zeek and Jim had hewed logs into beams with smooth sides for the floor. Zeek remembered how slow it had been to fit the logs together close enough for a floor. They had worked hard on it, trying to get finished before winter.

The floors of the cabins were about four inches above the porch floors and the walkway across the back. He was proud of the workmanship. It had held up for over thirty years.

Caleb Matthews had been gone about three weeks. Zeek had enjoyed the time spent with his dad. His mind was almost clear about who he was and the things in the past.

He watched the maple leaves falling from a tree into the water of Spring Branch. The water came from above the cabins and flowed underneath the bridge, built years earlier. The water flowed year-round. It always rose and flowed stronger in the fall, after the frost.

The leaves fluttered gently down as they fell into the stream. The bright yellow flashed in the sunlight as they floated in the ripples until they reached the first pool of water.

The water traveled faster just before it entered the pool. Zeek could not see any movement of the water while it was in the pool. He watched the leaves. Each one traveled at a different pace depending on how it landed in the water. Some stayed almost dry. They traveled fast through the rapids until they reached the pools. Those dry ones flowed across the pool before hanging up momentarily, then traveling fast again down the next rapids.

It was peaceful watching the water and the leaves flowing away from the cabin. It soothed his thoughts, and he was getting over the worry of the last two years.

After the bounty hunter came asking questions about him, Zeek had lived in fear of losing what he had. Again. He remembered each time before when things changed.

Zeek's worry had increased almost to a breaking point when the sheriff served the notice that he was being claimed by the Reynolds Plantation. He had never thought of himself as a runaway slave. Or even as property.

"How can I explain this to my family?" he had asked Jim Campbell when the papers were served.

Jim had suggested they just deny that he was Zeek.

Zeek never liked the idea of denying who he was, and did not intend to claim that he was Noel Milam.

He continued watching the leaves fall in the water, making stops in each little pool before going over and down the next rapids. He thought about the stages of his life, and the things he had gone through.

The first pool was like his childhood, when he lived with his mother and enjoyed the time before his dad went away. It was a serene period of time. While he wasn't but six years old when Caleb went away, he could remember the turmoil. It was like the rapids after the first pool.

The second period of time, after Caleb left, was like the rapids, and continued for a long time. Zeek thought about how hard it was to leave his mother. They were just beginning to recover from losing their dad. A short time later his grandfather took him and Ross away from their mother.

Zeek looked at the third set of rapids carrying the water toward Seiler's Creek. It was the roughest water in Spring Branch. The leaves he watched would go under and come back up. He watched as they reached the largest pool before the water crossed the road. That pool was like the last period of time, over the last thirty-five years.

He stood up and walked to the edge of the porch. He looked west across the valley at all the farmsteads that had been settled over the years. He never could relate his life before coming to the Campbell community with his life now. He had been too young to understand slavery and being a part of it.

While one memory would stand out as a pleasant vision in his mind, another one would cause a lump in his throat and tears to come to his eyes.

The vision of his mother watching when his grandfather took him away to be sold in New Orleans was the clearest of the bad memories Zeek could remember. He was almost ten years old. That memory haunted him more than any of the others.

He moved on to another memory: the day he went to the hearing. He had been afraid that he would never be able to return to sit on the porch again. That was almost as bad as the vision of his mother turning and dropping her head as the wagon pulled away for New Orleans. He also remembered his grandfather telling him and Ross not to look back.

"You're leaving, and you'll never see this place again." What his grandfather said had echoed through his mind ever since.

Zeek would never have the words to express the happiness he felt afterwards, when Mr. Hayes left the courtroom and returned with the $2000. He remembered the sound of Mr. Hayes' voice announcing the numbers as he laid the money on the bench in front of the judge.

Zeek did not fully understand what was happening until Mr. Hayes instructed the judge. When he said to make out a Bill of Sale from the plantation owner, Zeek realized something special was happening. When Mr. Hayes continued his instructions to make out the paper for Zeek's freedom, he understood. He had also felt numb as the transaction was finished.

After Mr. Hayes had received the paper for Zeek's freedom, he remembered what he had said to him.

"Follow me down to the clerk's office. We are going to record this paper. It says you are a free man. And you can take it home with you."

Zeek watched as the clerk of the court recorded the paper in the record.

He had continued walking and watching the leaves while his mind had reviewed the last few weeks.

The weeks following the hearing were filled with celebration. Zeek's freedom was special. He had just gotten used to who he was, and that he didn't have to live in fear anymore. And then he heard the fox horn.

After he heard the three sharp blasts of the fox horn, he walked toward the cabin, wondering what the emergency could be. His heart came up in his throat when he saw the sheriff sitting on the porch with a man he did not recognize.

When he saw they were laughing and were happy, he couldn't believe the sheriff would be laughing if there were a problem.

Vida came and met him and grabbed his right arm and shoulder. She whispered, "It's your daddy." She didn't hug him. She just walked with him to the porch where he met Caleb Matthews.

One of the leaves he had watched as it floated along Spring Branch made it across the gravel road and down the next set of rapids. It now floated peacefully in the bigger stream.

Zeek was like the leaf. He had made it through a lot of rough water. He had worked as a slave with no choice. He had worked as a laborer on the survey, but still wasn't making his own choices. He ran away and married Vida. He had lived a life of fear wondering what day he would be caught. He raised a family, and had almost gotten over the fear. He was accepted as part of the community. He was treated as an equal to everyone.

That peace had been shattered by the trial.

After all the things he had gone through, it was finally time for a real celebration. He was now entering another period of time in his life.

Zeek Matthews was now, Zeek Matthews a *free* man!

## ABOUT THE AUTHOR

Sam Pemberton was born on Bratton Creek, at an old homestead that hadn't changed much since the pioneer days. The year was 1944. Pemberton graduated from Big Flat high school. After their graduation in 1962, Sam married the love of his life, Patricia Treat.

He has worked construction in the drywall trade for most of his life. Sam presently lives in the beautiful Ozarks and continues in construction, as well as developing a new adventure called The Gathering Place in Big Flat, Arkansas, which is a restoration of the old building that is referred to in the novel as the store. He hopes you'll stop by sometime.